JOHN WORSLEY

The illustrations by John Worsley in the *Award Adventure Classics* series, have greatly added to the impact and charm of these dramatic stories. Now well-established as a portrait painter and marine artist, John Worsley was in the navy during the war. Taken prisoner, he and a fellow officer constructed an astonishingly life-like dummy to help in their escape plan. After the war he was appointed adviser to the makers of the famous war film, *Albert RN,* which tells the true story of this remarkable feat.

ISBN 0 86163 132 3

Award Publications Limited 1984
Spring House, Spring Place
London NW5, England

© 1982 Victoria House Publishing

Printed in Belgium

Mark Twain's
TOM SAWYER

Retold by Jane Carruth

AWARD PUBLICATIONS — LONDON

Aunt Polly

"TOM, TOM! Where are you?" There was no boy along the length and breadth of the Mississippi, who could disappear so completely as young Tom Sawyer. It was a mystery to his Aunt Polly how he did it. One minute he would be there beside her and the next he was gone – vanished into thin air!

The old lady pulled her spectacles down over her nose and looked over them, all round the room. Her spectacles were actually about as much use to her as a pair of saucepan lids but she cherished them above everything else. She searched the house to make sure that Tom was not hiding under the bed or in the cupboard; then she went outside and stood in the doorway. Lifting up her voice, she shouted, "Tom, Tom! Y-oou-u Tom!"

There was a sudden slight noise behind her, and she whirled round just in time to seize a small boy by his jacket.

"Where've you been? What have you been doing?" she demanded. "Look at your hands and mouth – all covered with jam!"

"Nothing, Aunt," mumbled Tom. Then, as she snatched up a switch, he cried, "Hey! Look behind you!"

The old lady grasped her skirts, dropping her switch as she did so, and Tom fled, scrambling up the broad high fence and disappearing quickly over the top in a second.

His Aunt Polly lowered her skirts and then began laughing gently. "Hang the boy!" she said aloud. "He's forever getting the better of me. But he's my own poor dead sister's son and I must do my best for him."

Truth to tell, the old lady loved Tom as if he was her own son and it worried her to death that he was by far the naughtiest, wildest boy in the village – with scarcely an atom of learning in his head. Not that Tom was stupid; he just couldn't see the point of wasting beautiful summer days – days that were fragrant with the scent of blossom – in the classroom.

Knowing that she had seen the last of him for the afternoon, the old lady went back to her knitting. But that night she quietly waited up for him and, as he climbed cautiously in at the window, she caught hold of him firmly. When she saw the state of his clothes, torn and dirty after a fight with another boy, she propped up her precious spectacles on top of her head for safety, and then gave him a good shake.

"Tomorrow is Saturday," she said. "But it'll be no holiday for you. It's hard labour you'll be doing – white-washing my fence. And not until it is all finished will you be free to play."

Tom groaned as he got up the next morning. Saturday! The day when he could go down to the river to watch the steamboats or hang round the village pump, talking and laughing with his friends. Instead, there was the fence to be whitewashed!

After breakfast, Aunt Polly, her face set and determined, gave him a bucket of whitewash and a long-handled brush. "Now, get on with it," she said firmly.

Tom sighed deeply as he looked up at the high broad fence. Then slowly he

dipped his brush into the bucket of whitewash and slowly he passed it along the topmost plank. He had hardly made any progress when a small coloured boy came skipping out of the gate carrying a tin pail.

"Hallo, Jim," Tom greeted the boy.

"Can't stop, Mastah Tom," was Jim's reply. "Missis tole me I got to go an git some water from the pump."

"Gimme the pail," said Tom, who suddenly saw a way of getting down to the village. "I'll fetch the water for you."

"Missis Polly will whack me," said Jim, rolling his eyes. "She'd take de head off me, she would!"

"Course she wouldn't," replied Tom. "Look, I'll give you my best marble."

Jim began to waver. He put down his pail and held out his hand for the treasure. The next minute, he was flying down the street with his pail and a tingling rear.

And Tom was whitewashing the fence as if his life depended on it. Aunt Polly smiled to herself as she retired from the scene, waving the slipper that she had just used on poor Jim, like a triumphant banner.

No sooner had his aunt disappeared into the house again, than Tom put down his brush. Searching in his pockets, he brought out his entire worldly wealth – some broken bits of toys, two marbles and a bent pin. There was simply nothing that would buy him more than ten minutes' freedom.

Then an idea came to him, an idea so brilliant that he whooped aloud. Once again he took up his brush, but this time his face bore the look of an artist who was doing exactly what he wanted to do. Out of the corner of his eye, he saw one of his hated rivals approach. It was Ben Rogers – one of the few boys who could make Tom mad by poking fun at him. Now, as he drew near, he held out the round red apple he was eating and called, "Hello, Tom, old friend! You got to work? Too bad and on Saturday, too!"

Tom went on whitewashing, paying no attention to anything but what he was doing. And at every gentle stroke of his brush, he smiled approvingly. To anyone who didn't know Tom very well indeed it looked as if he was really enjoying himself.

Ben tried again. "I'm going swimming. Don't you wish you could? But, of course, you'd rather work . . ."

"It all depends what you call work," Tom muttered.

"Why, what you're doing now, of course. That's work," returned Ben, looking slightly puzzled.

"All I know is, it suits Tom Sawyer," said Tom, gravely. "Why, it's not every day a boy gets a chance to whitewash a fence like this."

That put everything in a new light and Ben stopped nibbling his apple. Presently, he said, "Say, Tom, let me whitewash a little."

"No," said Tom, firmly, "I'm afraid I can't do that. You see Aunt Polly's very particular about this fence. It's got to be done very carefully. I reckon there's scarcely a boy in a thousand, maybe even two thousand, who can do it in the way it's got to be done."

"Is that so? Oh, come now, let me just try." Ben was in earnest now.

"Honest injun, Ben, I daren't . . ."

"I'll give you my apple," said Ben. "What's left of it, anyway."

Tom pretended to hesitate. Then, with a

doubtful look on his face but with great
glee in his heart, he gave Ben the brush.
And while Ben worked, Tom sat down on a
barrel in the shade, munching the apple
and planning the next step in his cam-
paign. By the time Ben was tired out, Tom
had traded the next glorious chance to
whitewash the fence to Billy Fisher for a
kite, and when he was exhausted, Johnny
Miller bought his chance for a dead rat
and a long piece of string.

By the middle of the afternoon, Tom had
more treasures than he had ever had in
his life. They included a tin soldier, a

couple of tadpoles, a kitten with only one eye, a brass door-knob and a knife handle. Besides all this glorious wealth, he had had a lovely lazy time, with plenty of company and the fence had been given no less than three coats of whitewash.

Aunt Polly was dozing by the open window when Tom presented himself later that same Saturday afternoon.

"May I go and play now, Aunt?" he asked. "The fence is all done."

"Tom, don't lie to me, I can't bear it," she said, wearily.

"I'm not lying. I tell you, it's all done," said Tom.

The old lady, placing small trust in Tom's words, went outside to see for herself. When she found the whole fence whitewashed and not only whitewashed once but coated, and recoated, her astonishment was so great that she almost lost her voice.

At last she exclaimed, "Well, I never! You can work when you've a mind to, Tom. Yes, go along and play. But mind you get back before it's dark, or I'll have to tan you."

And so overcome with the splendour of the fence was she, that she took Tom into the kitchen and gave him one of her juiciest apples, at the same time launching into a small sermon on the virtues of doing work honestly and well. And Tom, as he nodded and appeared to listen intently, managed to sneak a doughnut from the plate on the shelf and hide it away in his pocket, before finally escaping out of doors.

Tom goes to Sunday School

SUNDAY WAS a day which Tom would willingly have dropped from his week. For one thing it meant memorizing at least five verses of scripture. For another, it meant having his face and neck inspected by his cousin, Mary. And worst of all, it meant being forced to wear his "other clothes".

After breakfast, Aunt Polly held family worship at which Sidney, Tom's younger half-brother, was his usual model of good behaviour. When the prayers were over, Tom had to confess that unlike Sid, he had

not learnt his verses of scripture for Sunday school. From this chore there was positively no escape, and he was left alone for half-an-hour, after which Mary took his book to hear him recite the verses. Tom tried his best to find his way vainly through the fog.

"Oh, Tom, you poor thick-headed thing," Mary burst out, after listening to Tom's pathetic efforts. "You must go and learn it again. Don't be discouraged. You'll manage it – and if you do, I'll give you something ever so nice!"

"All right! What is it, Mary? Tell me what it is," Tom said, eagerly.

"Never you mind," replied Mary. "You know if I say it's nice, it is nice."

"All right, I'll try again then," said Tom a little less eagerly.

Tom did try it again; and under the double pressure of curiosity at Mary's present and the possible possession of it, he learnt his verses with such spirit that he achieved a shining success.

Mary gave him a brand-new "Barlow" knife, and the positive delight that swept through Tom at owning such a thing shook him to the core of his being. Then she produced a tin basin of water and a piece of soap, which Tom took outside the kitchen door. He set down the basin on a little bench; then he dipped the soap in the water and laid it down; turned up his sleeves; poured out the water on the ground gently; and then went back into the kitchen, and began to wipe his face diligently on the towel behind the door. But Mary took the towel from him and said, "Now, ain't you ashamed, Tom? You mustn't be so bad. Water won't hurt you."

Tom was a trifle put out at being so easily discovered. The basin was refilled, and this time he stood over it a little while, gathering determination. Then he took a big breath and began. When he returned to the kitchen after a little while, with both eyes shut, and groping for the towel with his hands, an impressive display of suds and water was dripping from his face. But when he emerged from the towel, he was still not scrubbed to her satisfaction.

The only thing for her to do was to take

him in hand herself, and when she was done with him he was a new man, shining and white, his saturated hair neatly brushed, so his short curls gave a dainty and symmetrical effect round his head. (He privately smoothed out the curls, and plastered his hair close down to his head. He thought curls were "girlish" and his own filled his life with misery.)

Satisfied at last with his appearance, Mary got out a suit of his clothing that had been used only on Sundays for the last two years. They were simply called his "other clothes", and by that we know the extent of his wardrobe!

After he had dressed himself, Mary buttoned his neat roundabout up to his chin, turned his vast shirt-collar down over his shoulders, brushed him off and crowned him with his speckled straw hat.

Tom now looked exceedingly improved and exceedingly uncomfortable. He hoped that Mary would forget his shoes but there was no such luck. At her insistence, he pushed his feet into them, snarling.

Sidney was already dressed and ready, and the three children set out together for Sunday-school – something that Tom hated with his whole heart, but which Sid and Mary both enjoyed.

Sunday-school hours were from nine to half past ten; after which there was the church service. Two of the children always remained for the sermon because they wanted to, and the other always remained because he was made to. The high-backed uncushioned pews would seat about three hundred people, and the church itself was a small, plain affair, with a sort of pine-board tree-box on top of it for a steeple.

As they went into Sunday-school Tom dropped back a step at the door and accosted a Sunday-dressed comrade.

"Say, Bill, got a yaller ticket?" he asked.

"Yes," was the reply.

"What'll you take for her?"

"What'll you give?"

"Piece of lickrish and a fish-hook."

"Let's see 'em."

Tom exhibited the generous offerings. They proved satisfactory to Bill and the property duly changed hands. Tom then began to waylay other boys as they arrived, and went on buying tickets of var-ious colours for as long as he could. Then he went into the church, walked over to his seat and started a quarrel with the first boy he could. The teacher, a grave, elderly man, tried to intervene, but Tom's whole class was so noisy and troublesome that the poor man had great difficulty in keeping any order at all.

Those members of his class who could struggle through the verses they had learnt were awarded with a small blue ticket. Ten blue tickets equalled a red one and could be exchanged for it; ten red tickets equalled a yellow one, and for ten yellow tickets the Superintendent gave a very plainly bound Bible to the pupil.

Only the older pupils managed to keep their tickets and stick to the tedious work long enough to get a Bible, and so the delivery of one of these prizes was a rare and noteworthy event. Tom had never really hungered for such a prize, but un-

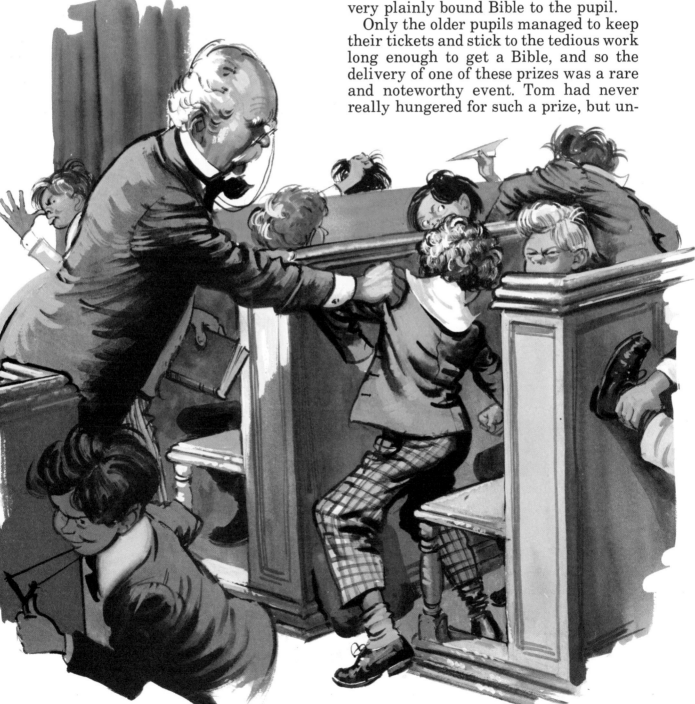

questionably his entire being longed for the glory that came with the presentation.

In due course the Superintendent stood up in front of the pulpit, with a closed hymn-book in his hand, his fore-finger inserted between its leaves, and commanded attention. He was a slim man of about thirty-five years old, with a sandy goatee beard, and short sandy hair. He wore a stiff standing-collar whose upper edge almost reached his ears, and whose sharp points curved forward, level with the corners of his mouth. His chin appeared to be propped on a spreading cravat, which was as broad and as long as a bank-note, and had fringed ends. His boot toes were turned sharply up, in the fashion of the day, like sleigh-runners. His name was Mr. Walters.

"Now, children," he began, "I want you all to sit up just as straight and pretty as you can. It does me good to see so many bright, clean little faces assembled in a place like this, learning to do right."

Except for incorruptible figures like Sid and Mary, all the pupils were fidgeting and whispering as the Superintendent launched into his favourite speech.

A good part of the whispering had been brought about by a rare event. Into the church had come Lawyer Thatcher, accompanied by a very feeble and elderly man, a fine, portly, middle-aged gentleman with iron-grey hair, and a dignified lady who was doubtless the latter's wife. The lady was leading a child, a very pretty girl with brilliant blue eyes and yellow hair plaited into two long tails. At the sight of her, Tom's soul was suddenly ablaze with fire, and the next moment he was "showing off" with all his might.

The visitors were given the highest seat of honour, and at the end of Mr. Walters' speech they were ceremoniously introduced to the school. The middle-aged man turned out to be a famous country judge, the great Judge Thatcher, who was the brother of their own lawyer. So great and unusual was the occasion felt to be that Mr. Walters began to "show off" too, with all sorts of official bustlings and activities. The librarian "showed off", running hither and thither with his arms full of books, and the young lady teachers

"showed off", bending sweetly over pupils, whom they would more normally box about the ears.

There was only one thing lacking to make Mr. Walters' ecstasy complete, and that was a chance to deliver a Bible-prize and thus exhibit a prodigy. Several pupils had yellow tickets, but none had the necessary ten.

Just at that moment when it seemed all hope was dead, Tom Sawyer came forward with nine yellow tickets, nine red tickets, and ten blue ones, and demanded a Bible! This was a thunderbolt out of a clear blue sky. Walters was not expecting an application from Tom of all people, for the next ten years, but there was no getting round

it. Tom was therefore elevated to a place with the Judge, and all the other boys were eaten up with envy as they watched.

The prize was delivered to Tom with as much enthusiasm as the Superintendent could muster under the circumstances. Alone among all the pupils, only little Amy Lawrence, who considered herself Tom's best girl, was glad and proud – that is until she saw Tom's adoring eyes on the pretty yellow-haired girl. Then she knew the worst: she had lost Tom forever, and she was so jealous and angry that she couldn't hold back the tears.

When Tom was finally introduced to the Judge, his breath would hardly come. His heart quaked, partly because of the awful greatness of the man, but mainly because he was *her* father. The Judge put his hand on Tom's head and called him a fine little man, and asked him his name.

The boy stammered, gasped, and finally managed to say, "Tom."

"Ah, Thomas! But you've got another name, too, I dare say, and you'll tell it to me, won't you?"

"Thomas Sawyer – sir," Tom replied.

"That's it! That's a good boy. Fine boy. Fine, manly little fellow. You will never be sorry for all the trouble you took to learn so many verses. Knowledge is worth more than anything else in the world. You'll be a great and good man yourself some day, Thomas. And now I'm sure you wouldn't mind telling me and this lady some of the things you've learned. No doubt you know the names of all the twelve disciples. So perhaps you will tell us the names of the first two?"

Tom was dumbfounded. He tugged at a button and looked miserable and sheepish. Then he blushed and his eyes fell. Mr. Walters' heart sank within him. Was it possible that the boy could not answer this simplest of questions, he asked himself. Why *did* the Judge ask him? He felt obliged to speak up.

"Answer the gentleman, Thomas – don't be afraid," he said.

Tom still hung fire.

"Now I know you'll tell *me*," said the lady. "The names of the first two disciples were . . . ."

"DAVID AND GOLIATH!"

Tom meets Huckleberry Finn

MONDAY MORNING found Tom Sawyer miserable. Monday always found him so, because it began another week's long suffering in school.

He lay and thought. And before long it occurred to him that he wished he was sick. He began to investigate the possibilities. When he discovered that one of his upper teeth was loose he considered himself in luck, until it occurred to him that his aunt would pull it out, and that would hurt.

No, he would keep the tooth in reserve and concentrate on something else. Then he remembered hearing the doctor tell about a certain something that laid up a patient for two or three weeks and threatened to make him lose a finger.

Tom had long ago forgotten the symptoms of the attack, but he decided that a sore toe might have some connection. So he began to groan with considerable spirit, at the same time clutching his toe.

But Sid slept on, unconscious.

Tom was annoyed. He called, "Sid, Sid!" and then he shook him. Sid's snores stopped. He yawned and stretched. Propping himself up on his elbow he stared at Tom. Tom went on groaning.

"Here, Tom! Tom! What's the matter?" Sid asked, looking anxious and stretching out a hand to him.

Tom moaned, "Oh, don't, Sid. Don't touch me!"

Thoroughly alarmed by now, Sid snatched up his clothes and flew downstairs.

"Oh, Aunt Polly, come quickly! Tom's dying!" he called as he ran.

"What's that? Rubbish. I don't believe it!" she said. But she flew upstairs with Sid and Mary at her heels. And her face was white and her lips trembled.

When she reached the bedside she gasped out, "Now, Tom! Tom, what's the matter with you?"

"Oh, Auntie, I'm – it's my sore toe, it's mortified!"

The old lady sank down into a chair and laughed a little, then cried a little, then did both together. This restored her, and she said, "Tom, what a turn you did give me. Now, you stop that nonsense and climb out of your bed."

The groans ceased, and Tom began to feel a little foolish.

"Aunt Polly, it *seemed* mortified, and it hurt so I never minded my tooth . . ."

"Your tooth, indeed! What's the matter with your tooth?"

"One of them's loose, and it aches perfectly awful."

"Well, your tooth *is* loose," declared Aunt Polly, after a quick look. "But you're not going to die from that. Mary, get me a silk thread, and a chunk of fire out of the kitchen."

Tom cried, "Oh, please, Auntie, don't pull it out. It doesn't hurt anymore, and I don't want to stay home from school."

"Oh, you don't, don't you? So all this row was because you thought you'd get off school and go fishing. Tom, I love you so, and yet you seem to try every way you can to break my old heart with your outrageousness."

By this time the dental instruments were ready. The old lady made one end of the silk thread fast to Tom's tooth with a loop, and tied the other end to the bedpost. Then she seized the chunk of fire and suddenly thrust it almost into Tom's face. In a twinkle the tooth hung dangling from the bedpost.

But all trials bring their compensations. As Tom walked to school after breakfast, he was the envy of every boy he met because the gap in his upper row of teeth enabled him to spit in a new and admirable way.

Before he reached school, Tom met the village lay-about, Huckleberry Finn, who was the son of the town drunkard. Huckleberry was cordially hated and dreaded by all the mothers of the town because he was idle, and lawless, and vulgar, and bad – and because all their children admired

him, and delighted in his forbidden company, and wished they dared be like him.

Tom was like the rest of the respectable boys in that he envied Huckleberry his romantic, outcast condition, and he, too, was under strict orders not to play with him. So he played with him every time he got a chance.

Huckleberry was always dressed in the cast-off clothes of full-grown men. His hat was a vast ruin with a wide crescent lopped out of its brim, and his coat (when he wore one) hung nearly to his heels. Only one brace supported his trousers, the seat of which bagged low and contained nothing. His trouser legs were fringed, and dragged in the dirt when not rolled up.

This disreputable appearance gave Huckleberry no concern at all. He slept on door-steps when it was fine, and in empty outhouses and sheds when it rained. He came and went as he pleased and did not have to go to school. He never had to wash, or wear clean clothes, and altogether, in Tom's eyes, he led a perfect life. It was therefore with considerable enthusiasm that Tom hailed his fortunate friend.

"Hallo, Huckleberry!"

"Hallo yourself, and see how you like it," retorted Huckleberry.

"What's that you got?"

"Dead cat."

"Lemme see him, Huck. My, he's pretty stiff. Where'd you get him?"

"Bought him off a boy."

"What did you give?"

"A blue ticket and a bladder that I got at the slaughter-house."

"Where'd you get the blue ticket?"

"Bought it off'n Ben Rogers two weeks ago for a hoopstick."

Tom digested this piece of information. Then he asked, "What is dead cats good for, Huck?"

"Good for? Cure warts with," said Huck knowingly.

"How d'you cure warts with cats?" inquired Tom, with disbelief in his voice.

"Why, you take your cat and go to the graveyard, round about midnight, where somebody that was wicked has been buried. And when it's midnight a devil will come, maybe two or three, but you can't see 'em, you can only hear something

like the wind, or maybe hear 'em talk; and when they're taking that feller away, you heave your cat after 'em and say, 'Devil follow corpse, cat follow devil, warts follow cat. I'm done with ye!' That'll cure *any* wart."

Tom thought for a minute. Then he said, "Sounds all right, Huck. When you going to try the cat?"

"Tonight. I reckon they'll come after old Hoss Williams tonight," Huck answered.

"Lemme go with you?" Tom asked eagerly.

"Of course – if you ain't afeard," was the somewhat sneering reply.

"Afeard! Tain't likely! Will you meow?"

"Yes, and you meow back if you get a chance," Huck told him.

And Tom, highly delighted at the prospect of an adventure with his friend, continued on his way to school.

When he reached the little isolated schoolhouse, he strode in briskly, with the manner of one who had come with all honest speed. He hung his hat on a peg, and flung himself onto his seat with business-like alacrity. The master, throned on high in his great, wooden armchair, was doz-

ing, and the interruption roused him.

"Thomas Sawyer!" he boomed, sternly.

Tom knew that when his name was pronounced in full, it meant trouble.

"Sir!"

"Come up here. Now, sir. As usual you are late. What is the reason this time?"

Tom was about to take refuge in a lie, when he saw two long tails of yellow hair hanging down a back that he recognized with the electric sympathy of pure love;

and by that form was *the only vacant place* over on the girls' side of the school-house.

He said instantly, "I STOPPED TO TALK WITH HUCKLEBERRY FINN!"

The master's pulse stood still, and he stared helplessly.

"Thomas Sawyer, this is the most astounding confession I've ever listened to," said the master. "Remove your jacket."

The master's arm performed until it was tired, and the pile of switches grew less and less. Then he gave the order, "Now, sir, go and sit with the *girls!*"

A titter rippled round the room, but Tom was only conscious of the worshipful awe he felt for his unknown idol as he sat down beside her, at the end of the bench.

Presently Tom began to steal furtive glances at the girl. She turned her head away, and when she cautiously faced around again, a peach lay before her. She thrust it away; Tom gently put it back. She thrust it away again, but with less determination than before. Tom patiently returned it to its place in front of her and she let it remain.

Then he began to draw something on his slate, hiding his work with his left hand. For a time, she took no notice. Then after a little while, curiosity overcame her and she whispered hesitatingly, "Let me see."

Tom partly uncovered a rather poor drawing of a house with two gable ends to it and a cork-screw of smoke issuing from the chimney.

She gazed at it for a moment, then whispered, "It's nice – make a man."

The artist obligingly placed a man in

the front garden. He could have stepped over the house, but the girl wasn't critical.

"It's a beautiful man – now make me."

Tom drew an hourglass, with a full moon and straw limbs to it. The girl said, "It's ever so nice – I wish I could draw."

"It's easy," whispered Tom. "I'll learn you. What's your name?"

"Becky Thatcher."

"And I'm Tom Sawyer." As he spoke, Tom began to scrawl something on the slate, hiding the words from Becky.

At her entreaties, Tom began letting his hand slip by degrees away from the slate till what he had written was clearly revealed. It said, "I love you."

"Oh, you bad thing!" Becky exclaimed. And she hit his hand a smart rap, but reddened and looked pleased anyway.

When school broke up at noon, Tom turned to Becky Thatcher, and whispered in her ear, "Put on your bonnet and pretend you're going home. Then when you get to the corner, give the rest of 'em the slip, and turn down through the lane and

come back. I'll go the other way, and pretend I'm going home too."

Becky nodded, and in a little while the two met at the bottom of the lane. They walked together back towards the schoolhouse and when they reached it they found it was quite deserted. Then they sat, side-by-side, with a slate before them, and Tom gave Becky the pencil. He held his hand over hers, guiding it, and so created another surprising house.

Presently Tom asked, "Becky, was you ever engaged?"

"What's that?"

"Why, engaged to be married."

"No."

"Would you like to?"

Becky nodded, and Tom passed his arm about her waist and whispered his words of love into her ears.

"It's ever so much fun being engaged," he said. "Why me and Amy Lawrence – "

Becky's eyes widened, and Tom realized his blunder, but it was too late. Becky began to cry and as her sobs grew louder,

he got out his most prized jewel, a brass knob from the top of a fire-guard.

"Please, Becky, take this."

She struck it to the floor. At that, Tom stood up and marched out of the schoolhouse – over the hills and far away, to return to school no more that day.

"Tom! Come back, Tom!" Becky entreated through her tears. And when he did not, she sat down and cried again.

Tom's midnight adventure

TOM SPENT the rest of the day in the woods, and by the time he got back home, his broken heart was well on the way to being repaired.

At half-past nine that night, he and Sid were sent to bed as usual. They said their prayers, and Sid was soon asleep. Tom lay

awake for a while, tossing in restless impatience, but, inspite of himself, he began to doze. When the clock chimed eleven, he did not hear it.

Suddenly, mingling with his half-formed dreams, he heard a most melancholy caterwauling. The crash of an empty bottle against the back-door of his aunt's wood-shed made sure he was wide awake; less than a minute later he was dressed and out of the window, creeping along the low roof of the kitchen on all fours. He "meow'd" with caution once or twice as he went. Then he jumped to the roof of the wood-shed, and thence to the ground where Huckleberry Finn was waiting for him, with his dead cat. Half-an-hour later they were wading through the tall grass of the graveyard.

It was a graveyard of the old-fashioned western kind, set on a hill, some way away from the village. It had a crazy board-fence around it, which leaned inward in places, and outward in others, actually standing upright nowhere. A wilderness of grass and weeds grew over the whole cemetery, and all the old graves were sunken into the ground.

A faint wind moaned through the trees, and Tom feared it might be the spirits of the dead complaining at being disturbed. He was thankful when they came upon the sharp new heap of earth they were looking for, and soon they were hidden by the three great elms that grew in a bunch just next to this grave.

They waited in silence until, suddenly, Tom seized Huck's arm and said, "Ssh!"

The two clung together with beating hearts and Huckleberry whispered nervously, "What is it, Tom?"

"Ssh! There 'tis again. Didn't you hear it?" Tom said.

"Lord, Tom, they're coming! They're coming, sure as anything. What'll we do? They can see in the dark, same as cats . . ."

The boys bent their heads together and scarcely breathed. A muffled sound of voices floated up from the far end of the graveyard.

"Look! See there!" whispered Tom. "What is it?"

"It's devil-fire. Oh, Tom, this is awful," groaned Huckleberry.

Some vague figures approached through the gloom, swinging an old-fashioned tin lantern that freckled the ground with innumerable little spangles of light. Huckleberry whispered with a shudder, "It's the devils, sure enough. Three of 'em. Lordy, Tom, we're goners! Can you pray?"

"I'll try, but don't you be afeard," Tom whispered back.

Then Huck exclaimed softly, "They're *humans!* One of 'em is, anyway. One of 'em is old Muff Potter's voice."

Tom listened intently. "Say, Huck, I know another o' them voices – it's Injun Joe," he said.

"That's so – that murderin' half-breed! I'd rather they was devils," muttered Huck. "What can they be up to?"

By now the three men had reached the grave, and were standing very close to the boys' hiding-place.

"Here it is," said the third voice; and the owner of it held the lantern up to reveal the face of young Dr. Robinson.

Potter and Injun Joe were carrying a hand-barrow with a rope and a couple of shovels on it. They put this on the ground and began to open the grave. While they were working, the doctor put the lantern at the head of the grave, and sat down with his back against an elm tree. He was

so close the boys could have touched him.

"Hurry, men!" he said in a low voice. "The moon might come out."

They growled a response and went on digging. Finally, one of them struck upon the coffin with a dull, woody noise. The men hoisted it out on the ground. They prised off the lid with their shovels, got out the body and dumped it rudely on the ground. Just at that moment, the moon drifted out from behind the clouds and exposed the pallid face. The barrow was got ready and the corpse placed on it, covered with a blanket, and bound in place with the rope. Then Potter took out a spring-knife and cut off the end of the rope.

"Now the cussed thing's ready, Sawbones," he said. "And you'll just out with another five, or here she stays."

"That's the talk!" said Injun Joe.

"Look here; what does this mean?" said the doctor. "You required your pay in advance, and I've paid you."

"Yes, and you done more than that," said Injun Joe, approaching the doctor.

"Five years ago you drove me away from your father's kitchen one night when I come to ask for something to eat. When I swore I'd get even with you if it took a hundred years, your father had me jailed for a tramp. Did you think I'd forget? The Injun blood ain't in me for nothing. And now I've got you, and you got to settle!"

He was threatening the doctor with his fist in his face by this time. The doctor struck out suddenly, and stretched the ruffian on the ground.

"Here, no, don't you strike my pard!" Potter exclaimed, dropping the knife on the ground. The next moment he was grappling with the doctor, and the two were struggling with might and main.

Injun Joe sprang to his feet, his eyes flaming with passion as he snatched up Potter's knife, and began to creep catlike, stooping round and round about the combatants, seeking an opportunity.

Suddenly the doctor flung himself free, seized the heavy headboard of the grave and felled Potter to the ground with it. In

the same instant the half-breed saw his chance, and drove the knife to its hilt in the young man's breast. The doctor reeled and fell across Potter, covering him with his blood. In the same moment the clouds blotted out the dreadful spectacle, and the two frightened boys went speeding away in the dark as fast as they could.

When the moon emerged again, Injun Joe was standing over the two forms. The doctor murmured something then gave a long gasp or two, and was still.

"That score is settled, damn you!" muttered the half-breed.

Quickly he robbed the doctor's body of all its belongings and after that he put the fatal knife in Potter's open right hand. Then he sat down on the dismantled coffin. Three – four – maybe five minutes passed, before Potter began to stir and moan. His hand closed upon the knife, and he held it up and look at it. Instantly he let it fall with a shudder and sat up, pushing the body from him. He gazed at it and then around him in a confused manner.

"It's a dirty business," said Joe, without moving. "What did you do it for?"

"Me! I never done it," replied Potter.

"That kind of talk won't wash," Joe said.

Potter trembled and grew white. "I didn't know what I was a-doing," he muttered. It must have been all that whisky I drunk. You won't tell, will you, Joe?" And the poor creature dropped on his knees before the real murderer, in an appeal.

"No, you've always been fair and square with me, Muff Potter, and I won't go back on you," said Joe.

"Oh, Joe, bless you!" Potter cried.

"Come, man," said Injun Joe. "No blubbering. You be off yonder way and I'll go this. Don't leave any tracks behind you."

Meanwhile Tom and Huck were running on and on towards the village, speechless with horror, and terrified that they might be followed.

"If we can only get to the old tannery before we break down!" whispered Tom, in short catches between breaths.

When at last they burst through the tannery's open door, they were too exhausted to speak for a while.

Finally Tom whispered, "What do you reckon'll come of it?"

Huck Finn and Tom Sawyer swears they will keep mum about this and they wish they may Drop down dead in their tracks if they ever tell and Rot.

T.S.   H.F.

"If Dr. Robinson dies, I reckon hanging'll come of it," retorted Huck.

Tom thought awhile, then he said, "Who'll tell? Us?"

"What are you talking about?" Huck burst out. "If something happened and Injun Joe didn't hang, why he'd kill us some time or other, just as dead sure as we're a-lying here."

After some reflective silence, Tom said, "Huck, you sure you can keep mum?"

"Tom, we got to keep mum," replied his friend gravely. "That Injun devil wouldn't make any more of drowning us than a couple of cats. There orter be writing 'bout a big thing like this. And blood."

Tom's whole being applauded the idea. He picked up a clean block of pine wood that lay in the moonlight, and took a little fragment of ochre dye out of his pocket.

Then he painfully scrawled their oath.

Each boy pricked the ball of his thumb and squeezed out a drop of blood. Tom showed the admiring Huckleberry how to make an H and an F, after he had signed his own initials, and the oath was complete. They buried the shingle close to the wall, with ceremony and wailed incantations. Then the fetters that bound their tongues were considered to be locked and the key thrown away.

Tom runs away

THE WHOLE village was horrified by the ghastly news of the young doctor's murder. A gory knife had been found close to the murdered man, and it had been identified as belonging to Muff Potter.

Tom joined the procession that began drifting towards the graveyard; and so, too, did Huckleberry Finn. The boys shivered when their eyes fell on the stolid face of Injun Joe. The crowd fell apart as the sheriff came through leading Potter by the arm. The poor fellow's face was haggard, and his eyes showed the fear that was upon him.

"I didn't do it, friends," he sobbed. And when his eyes lighted on Injun Joe, he shouted, "Tell 'em, Joe, tell 'em!"

Huckleberry and Tom stood dumbfounded and staring as they heard the stony-hearted liar reel off his statement about the fight, with never a word about his own terrible part in it.

At the inquest, which followed, Injun Joe repeated his statement under oath, just as calmly, and Muff Potter was thrust into jail to await trial.

Tom's conscience was deeply troubled, and every day or two, whenever he had the opportunity, he went to the little grated jail window and smuggled such small comforts through to the "murderer" as he could get hold of. The jail was a trifling little brick den that stood in a marsh at the edge of the village, and there were no guards, so Tom's efforts to ease his conscience went undiscovered.

Soon, however, the fate of poor Muff Potter was no longer his prime concern.

Becky Thatcher had stopped coming to school, and Tom could not find out what had happened to her. He grew more and more melancholy and pale and dejected. Aunt Polly was very worried about him and tried every cure she knew to bring the colour back into his cheeks, but all to no avail. Tom remained morose.

Then one day, as he hung about the gate of the school-yard instead of playing with his comrades, he saw her! His heart gave a great bound, and the next instant he was "showing-off", yelling, laughing, chasing boys, and jumping over the fence at risk of life and limb. But Becky did not spare him a glance. Tom continued to war-whoop around, then he snatched a boy's cap, hurled it to the roof of the schoolhouse, broke through a group of boys, and fell, sprawling, under Becky's nose.

She turned away from him, with her nose in the air, and he heard her say, "Mmf! Some people think they're mighty smart – always showing off!"

Tom's cheeks burned. He gathered himself up and sneaked off, crushed and crestfallen. His mind was now made up. He was forsaken and friendless. Nobody loved him. He would run away.

He set off down Meadow Lane, and after a while he heard the bell for school, tinkling faintly in the distance. At that point he began to sob, and soon the sobs were coming thick and fast.

Just then he met his soul's sworn comrade, Joe Harper. Joe, too, was miserable and dejected, having been punished unjustly by his mother for a crime he vowed he had not committed.

As the two boys walked along the riverbank, they began to make plans. A short distance below St. Petersburg, at a point where the Mississippi River was very wide, there was a long, narrow, wooded island, with a shallow bar at the head of it, which would offer an ideal rendezvous. It was not inhabited; it lay far over towards the further shore, and to get to it a dense and almost wholly unpopulated forest had to be crossed. The boys agreed that they should become pirates and live a life of crime, and this place – Jackson's Island – was the chosen spot for their headquarters.

This settled, they hunted up Huckleberry Finn, who promptly joined them. Then the three separated; they would meet again at a lonely spot on the river bank, at the magic hour of midnight.

It was starlight, and very still, when Tom arrived with a boiled ham and a few trifles at the appointed meeting place. The mighty river lay like an ocean at rest, and Tom listened a moment before giving a low, distinct whistle. It was answered from the darkness below. Tom whistled twice more, and these signals were answered in the same way. Then a guarded voice said, "Who goes there?"

"Tom Sawyer, the Black Avenger of the Spanish Main. Name your names," said Tom gravely.

"Huck Finn the Red-handed, and Joe Harper the Terror of the Seas," came the reply.

"'Tis well. Give the countersign."

Two hoarse whispers delivered the same awful word simultaneously: "BLOOD!"

Then Tom tumbled his ham down to his waiting comrades and let himself down after it, tearing both skin and clothes in the effort. There was an easy, comfortable path along the shore of the river, but it lacked the advantages of difficulty and danger, so valued by pirates.

The Terror of the Seas had brought a side of bacon, and Finn the Red-handed had stolen a skillet, and a quantity of half-cured leaf tobacco, and had also brought a few corn-cobs to make pipes with. However, none of the pirates but himself smoked or "chewed". The Black Avenger of the Spanish Main said it would never do to start without some fire, which was a wise thought, and they saw a fire

smouldering upon a great raft a little distance away. They crept stealthily down to it and helped themselves to a chunk, making the enterprise a daring adventure.

Then they shoved off, Tom in command, Huck at the after oar and Joe at the for'ard. Tom stood amidships, gloomy-browed, and with folded arms, and gave his orders in a low, stern whisper.

Their raft drew beyond the middle of the river; the boys pointed her head right, and then really pulled on their oars. As they passed before the distant town, all three pirates felt that they were seeing it for the last time.

About two o'clock in the morning the raft grounded on the bar just above the head of the island, and the intrepid pirates waded back and forth until they had landed their freight. Part of the little raft's belongings consisted of an old sail, and this they spread over a nook in the bushes for a tent to shelter their provisions. They themselves would sleep in the open air, as became outlaws.

They built a fire against the side of a great log a short distance inside the dark forest, and then cooked some bacon in the frying-pan for supper. It seemed glorious sport to be feasting in that wild free way in

the forest and on an island far from the haunts of men.

"This is just the life for me," said Tom. "You don't have to get up mornings, and you don't have to go to school, and wash, and all that blame foolishness. You see, Joe, a pirate don't have to do *anything*."

Joe declared himself perfectly satisfied at being a pirate, and Huck presently began to blow out a cloud of fragrant smoke from his cob pipe. Then he asked, "What does pirates have to do?"

"Oh, they just have a bully-time," Tom said. "They take ships, and burn them, and get the money and bury it in awful places in their island where there's ghosts and things to watch it, and kill everybody in the ships – make 'em walk a plank."

As they talked, the pipe dropped from the fingers of the Red-handed, and he slept. But the Terror of the Seas and the Black Avenger of the Spanish Main had more trouble in getting to sleep. They began to feel a vague fear that they had been doing wrong to run away. Next they thought of the stolen meat; there was a command against stealing in the Bible. So they inwardly resolved that as long as they remained pirates, they would not commit the crime of stealing. And once this resolution was taken, they fell peacefully to sleep.

Early the next morning Tom stirred up the other pirates, who were soon awake. In a minute or two they were all stripped and they chased after and tumbled over

each other in the shallow limpid water of the white sand-bar.

Breakfast cooked on their camp fire was a gratifying affair, and then there was the whole day left to explore the island. But as the day wore on, the stillness and solemnity that brooded in the woods began to tell upon the spirits of the pirates. It was the beginning of home-sickness, but they were all too ashamed of their weakness to actually voice their thoughts.

Late in the afternoon, a muffled boom startled all three of them, and they sprang to their feet and ran to the shore. They parted the bushes on the bank and peered out over the water. They saw the little steam ferry-boat some way below the village, drifting with the current. Her broad deck seemed crowded with people, and there were a great many skiffs rowing about or floating with the stream in the neighbourhood of the ferry-boat. Presently a great jet of white smoke burst from the ferryboat's side.

"I know what it's all about," Tom suddenly exclaimed. "Somebody's drownded!"

"That's it," said Huck. "They shoot a cannon over the water and that makes the drownded man come up to the top . . ."

The boys watched intently. Then Tom suddenly cried, "Boys, I know who's drownded: it's us!"

The pirates returned to camp, full of vainglory at the trouble they were making, but when the shadows of night closed them in, their excitement vanished, and Tom and Joe could not keep back thoughts of certain people at their homes who were not enjoying this fine frolic as much as they were. Presently Huck and Joe fell asleep, but Tom did not. At last he rose cautiously: he had something to do.

It was broad daylight before Tom once again reappeared at the camp site. Over a sumptuous breakfast of bacon and fish, he recounted his adventures. He had sneaked back home and had witnessed the grief of Aunt Polly and Joe's mother who believed they were all "drownded".

Tom's exploit was daring enough to keep the gang in high spirits for the rest of the day. But the next day, Joe was far from cheerful. He sat poking up the sand with a stick, and looking very gloomy. Finally he said, "Oh, let's give it up. I want to go home. It's so lonesome."

"Well, we'll let the cry-baby go home to his mother, won't we, Huck?" said Tom.

And Huck said, "Y-e-s" – without any heart in it.

And when Tom saw at last how it was with the two bold pirates, he let them into the secret plan he had been making. So outrageous and spectacular was it that his companions were won over instantly.

"We'll stay," said Joe. "It's only a day or two longer anyway."

Tom's great plan was to return home with his brother pirates and attend their own funerals which, he had learnt on his expedition, were to take place on the following Sunday.

Accordingly, at dusk on the Saturday, they paddled over to the Missouri shore on a log, and slept in the woods on the edge of the town till nearly daylight. Then they made their way to the unused gallery of the church to await events.

As the bell began to toll, instead of ringing in the usual ·way, the villagers

crowded into the little church. Then Aunt Polly entered, followed by Sid and Mary, and then by the Harper family, all in deep black. The whole congregation, the old minister as well, rose reverently and stood, until the mourners were seated in the front pew.

As the service proceeded, there was a rustle in the gallery which nobody noticed; a moment later the church door creaked. The minister, overcome by his own moving words, raised his streaming eyes above his handkerchief. As he stared at the door he stopped talking, but his mouth remained wide open. And then, almost with one impulse, the congrega-tion turned and stared while the three dead boys came up the aisle – Tom in the lead, Joe next, and Huck, a ruin of droop-ing rags, sneaking sheepishly in the rear.

Aunt Polly, Mary and the Harpers threw themselves upon their restored ones, smothering them with kisses, while poor Huck stood abashed and uncomfort-able. As he started to slink away, Tom seized him.

"Aunt Polly, it ain't fair," he cried. "Somebody's got to be glad to see Huck."

"And so they shall!" cried Aunt Polly. But the loving attentions the old lady now lavished upon the outcast made him even more uncomfortable than he had been!

Buried treasure

FOR THE REMAINDER of the school term, Tom was the hero of the hour. He did not skip or prance about, but moved with a dignified swagger as became a pirate who felt that the public eye was upon him.

It is true that the object of his undying love did not immediately restore him to favour. But as the holidays drew near Becky Thatcher smiled on him again, and the two were happily re-united.

Only one thing marred Tom's otherwise long, happy, carefree days away from school. This was Muff Potter's trial for murder. He hung about the court-room, unable to tear himself away, and when at last he was convinced that poor Muff Potter would be found guilty, he asked to be called as witness for the defence.

The sight of Injun Joe's iron face made Tom shiver but, somehow or other, he got started on his story. As he warmed to his subject, the audience hung upon his words.

Then Tom said, "And as the doctor swung the board around and Muff Potter fell, Injun Joe jumped with the knife and . . . ."

Crash! Quick as lightning, the half-breed sprang from his seat, tore his way through all opposers and was gone!

Tom was a glittering hero once more, but his dreams were haunted by Injun Joe coming to take his revenge, and he wished with all his heart that he could be captured.

The long lazy days drifted on. Becky went away on holiday, and Tom turned his mind to other matters. Hidden treasure was one.

"We'll dig for it on Cardiff Hill," he said to Huck, one morning, "under the old dead tree that stands there on the top."

Huck was delighted with the diversion and, armed with a rusty old pick and a

shovel, the two set out on their tramp to the site.

On the days that followed, they dug a number of holes without finding as much as an old bone, and many a time, Tom cast a long and thoughtful look on the crumbling, derelict house in the Valley below. It had the dread, but fascinating reputation of being haunted.

On Saturday they returned again to the dead tree. They dug a little in the last hole

they had made, but with no great hope. Then they shouldered their tools and went down the hill towards the haunted house.

When they reached it, there was something so weird and grisly about the dead silence that reigned there under the baking sun, that they were afraid for a moment to venture in. Then they crept to the door and took a trembling peep. They saw a weed-grown floorless room, unplastered, an ancient fire-place, and a ruinous staircase. All around hung ragged cobwebs.

Wondering at their own boldness, they entered softly and then, daring each other, they threw their tools into a corner and went upstairs. Their courage was up now, and well in hand. Finding nothing of interest though, they were about to go down again when Tom suddenly said, "Ssh!"

"What is it?" whispered Huck, blanching with fear.

"Ssh! There! Hear it? Keep still. They're coming right towards the door downstairs," Tom said softly.

The boys stretched themselves upon the floor with their eyes to knot-holes in the planking, and lay waiting in a cloud of fear.

Two men entered, and each boy said to himself, "There's the old Spaniard that's been seen in the town lately."

The Spaniard was wrapped in a blanket. He had bushy white whiskers; long white hair flowed from under his sombrero, and he wore green goggles. His companion was not clearly visible until he spoke, but when he did, the boys gasped and quaked even more. It was the voice of Injun Joe! As they watched and listened it became clear that Injun Joe had some vengeful plan which he meant to carry out before finally leaving the district and escaping to Texas.

As the sun was setting, the two men began talking about burying their swag, "six hundred and fifty in silver", and the boys forgot all their fears as they saw Joe, on his knees, in the corner digging with his bowie-knife. They nudged each other in their gloating excitement.

Suddenly Joe's knife struck something.

"Hallo," he said. "Here's a half-rotten plank – no, it's a box. I've broke a hole."

He reached his hand in and drew it out.
"Man, it's money!" he exclaimed.

The two villains examined the gold coins, and the Spaniard said, "We'll make swift work of this. I just saw an old pick."

He ran and brought over Tom's pick and shovel. Very soon the box was unearthed. It was iron-bound, not very large, and had been very strong before the slow years had rotted it. Joe said, "There's thousands of dollars here."

"Must have been old Murrel's gang," said his companion.

"We'll take it to our den – number two, under the cross," said Injun Joe.

As they slipped out of the house in the deepening twilight, Tom and Huck rose up, weak but vastly relieved. They had escaped detection. Now all they had to do was to track down the iron-bound box and the treasure would be theirs!

In the days that followed, Tom made a hundred and one plans as to how to track down the iron-bound box. But then something happened that made Injun Joe and the treasure become less important.

Becky was home again. Judge Thatcher had chartered an old ferry-boat and a picnic would be held for her friends down river on Friday.

Tom was in a fever of excitement, when Friday morning dawned, clear and bright.

"I tell you what," he said to Becky, as they tripped along. "We'll climb Cardiff Hill and then we'll stop at Widow Douglas's place. She'll have ice-cream, and she'll be awfully glad to have us. She'll be glad to put us both up at the end of the picnic and that'll save you spending the night at the Harper's like your Ma said."

Becky agreed somewhat doubtfully, as they boarded the ferry. Sometime later the crowd of laughing boys and girls swarmed ashore, and after some games, a feast was spread out and devoured in the shade of spreading oaks.

Presently somebody shouted, "Who's ready for the cave?"

Everybody was, and as bundles of candles were produced, there was a general scamper up the hill. The mouth of McDougal's Cave was high up the hillside, and made an opening shaped like an A. Its massive oaken door stood unbarred.

Within was a small chamber, as chilly as an ice-house. McDougal's Cave was, in fact, a vast labyrinth of crooked aisles that ran into each other and out again and led nowhere. Most of the young men knew a portion of it, and Tom knew as much of the cave as anyone.

With Becky at his side, Tom followed the rest. They did not immediately notice that they had wandered off and were alone. On and on they went, far down into the cave's secret depths until, finally, they found themselves in a cavern, the walls of which were supported by many pillars.

Under the roof thousands of bats had packed themselves, and as the light from the candles disturbed them, they came flocking down, squeaking furiously. They darted at the candles, and Becky's went out. Thoroughly frightened, the children ran into every new passage they found. And now for the first time the deep stillness of the place laid clammy hands on them. Becky shivered.

"We'd better start back, Tom," she whispered. "I hope we won't get lost."

But the bats had chased them a good distance and before long Tom knew, with sinking heart, they were hopelessly lost.

They began wandering aimlessly then

until they came upon a spring. Worn out and hungry, Becky sank to the ground.

"They're sure to miss us soon," Tom comforted her. Then he remembered that her mother thought she was spending the night at the Harper's house, and his courage all but ebbed away.

The weary time dragged on; they slept a little, and awoke famished and woe-stricken: then slept again. Then suddenly an idea struck him. It would be better to explore some of the side-passages than sit helplessly waiting. He took a length of string from his pocket, tied it to a projection, and he and Becky started, Tom in the lead, unwinding the string as he groped along. At the end of twenty steps the corridor ended in a "jumping-off" place. Tom got down on his knees and felt below, and then as far around the corner as he could.

He made a great effort to stretch just a little farther to the right, and at that moment, hardly any distance away, a human hand, holding a candle, appeared from behind a rock! Tom's joyous shout faded on his lips as he saw the body that followed the hand: it belonged to – Injun Joe! For a moment he was paralyzed. Then to his intense relief, he realized that the half-breed had not seen him, and return-

ing quickly to Becky, he led her back to the spring without giving her a hint of what he had seen.

The third passage Tom tried rewarded him beyond his wildest hope. There, far-off, was a speck that looked like daylight. He groped forward, pushed his head and shoulders through a small hole, and saw the broad Mississippi rolling by.

Half-dead with hunger and weariness, Becky allowed herself to be pushed along the passage and helped through the hole. Then some men came along in a skiff, and Tom hailed them. As night fell, the two children, who had been given up for lost, were safely back home, and the whole village went mad with joy.

When Becky was sufficiently recovered to give her own account of the story, Tom came out of it so well that he was a hero.

Huckleberry, too, was enjoying something akin to hero worship for, on that momentous day of the picnic, he had come upon Injun Joe and the Spaniard, and creeping up on them had learnt more of Joe's plan to wreak vengeance on the Widow Douglas. It seemed that, long ago, her husband had caused the half-breed to be publicly horse-whipped, and Injun Joe had determined to wipe out the insult. Huck had raised the alarm. The villains had escaped – at least Joe had. The other, the white-bearded Spaniard, had drowned in the river. Out of gratitude, the widow had taken Huck into her own house.

All this Tom learnt with some considerable amazement. But it was only later – two whole weeks later – that he learnt something else that drove the colour from his cheeks and left him white and trembling.

On his way to visit Huck, he stopped at Judge Thatcher's house to see Becky, and the judge said to him, "Well, Tom, nobody will get lost in that cave anymore. I've had its door sheathed with iron two weeks ago, and triple locked; and I've got the keys."

And Tom, nearly fainting away, at last found the strength to mutter, "Oh, Judge, Injun Joe's in the cave!"

The treasure-seekers strike gold

WITHIN AN amazingly short time, the news had spread and soon a dozen skiff-loads of men, including Judge Thatcher and Tom, were on their way to McDougal's Cave. When the cave door was unlocked, a sorrowful sight presented itself in the dim twilight of the place. Injun Joe lay stretched upon the ground, dead, with his face close to the crack of the door and, by his side, was his knife, its blade broken in two. Tom, at the sight of him, felt a touch of pity mingled with a vast sense of relief.

Injun Joe was buried near the mouth of the cave and, after the funeral, Tom took Huck aside.

"Huck," he said, "I know where the money is. It's in the cave."

"It's a long way in," Tom continued, "but there's a mighty short cut that nobody knows about but me. Will you come, Huck?"

"Let's start right off, Tom," Huck said.

Soon after noon, the boys borrowed a small skiff and got under way. When they had journeyed some way, Tom broke the heavy silence with the words, "Do you see that white place up yonder where there's been a landslide? Well, that's one of my landmarks. We'll get ashore now."

They landed, and Tom proudly showed Huck the hole among the thick bushes which had been the means of his and Becky's escape from the cave.

Then they entered, Tom in the lead. They toiled their way to the farther end of the tunnel, and a few steps more brought them to the spring. Tom shuddered at the sight of it. They pressed on, and soon entered and followed Tom's other corridor until they reached the "jumping-off" place. Their candles revealed that it was not really a precipice, but only a steep hill.

Tom held his candle aloft and said, "Now, Huck, look as far around the corner as you can. Look on the big rock over yonder – marked with candle smoke."

"Oh, it's a *cross*!" exclaimed Huck.

"Exactly right," said Tom. "It's *the* cross where Injun Joe buried the money box."

At the foot of the clay hill, they came upon a small recess in one of the avenues close to the base of the great rock. This held some blankets, an old pair of braces, and the well-gnawed bones of two or three fowls. But there was no money box.

Then Tom said, "I bet you the money is *under* the rock. I'm going to dig in the clay."

His knife was out at once, and he had hardly begun to dig when he struck wood. So he uncovered some boards, which Huck helped him to remove. They had concealed a natural chasm which led under the rock. Tom got into this, and held his candle as far under the rock as he could. He followed its winding course, with Huck close at his heels, and suddenly he exclaimed, "My goodness, Huck, looky here!"

It was the treasure-box sure enough, occupying a snug little cavern along with an empty powder-keg, a couple of guns in

leather, two or three pairs of old moccasins, a leather belt, and some other rubbish well soaked by the dripping water.

"Got it at last," said Huck, ploughing among the tarnished coins with his hands. "My, but we're rich, Tom!"

Tom and Huck's windfall, all of twelve thousand dollars, made a mighty stir in the poor little village of St. Petersburg. The money was carefully invested for them, but each lad now had an enormous income – a dollar for every week-day in the year and half of the Sundays.

Huck Finn's wealth, and the fact that he was now under the Widow Douglas's protection, introduced him into society – and his sufferings were almost more than he could bear, for he was combed and brushed daily. He had to eat with a knife and fork, learn his books, and go to church.

"No, Tom," said he, one day. "I've made up my mind. I won't be rich. I won't live in them cussed smothery houses. I like the woods, and the river, and the hogshead. The widder's good to me, and friendly, but

I can't stand her ways. No, Tom, I won't be rich. Blame it all! Just as we'd got guns, and a cave, and all just fixed to rob, here this dern foolishness has got to come up and spoil it all!"

Tom saw his chance. "Look here, Huck, being rich ain't going to keep me back from turning robber."

"No! Are you in real dead-wood earnest, Tom?"

"Sure I am, but we can't let you into the gang if you ain't respectable, Huck."

Huck's joy was quenched.

"A robber is more high-toned than what a pirate is," Tom told him. "In most countries they're awful high up in the nobility – dukes and such. So you see, Huck, you'd have to be respectable."

So Huck was won over, and Tom Sawyer's story must end with Huckleberry's fervent promise. "I'll stick to the widder," said he, "till I rot, Tom; and if I git to be a reg'lar ripper of a robber, and everybody talking 'bout it, I reckon she'll be proud she took me in out of the wet."